A

André Alexis

BookThug

2013

FIRST EDITION

copyright © André Alexis, 2013

The production of this book was made possible through the
generous assistance of The Canada Council for the Arts
and The Ontario Arts Council.

Canada Council   Conseil des Arts
for the Arts   du Canada

ONTARIO ARTS COUNCIL
CONSEIL DES ARTS DE L'ONTARIO

50 YEARS OF ONTARIO GOVERNMENT SUPPORT OF THE ARTS
50 ANS DE SOUTIEN DU GOUVERNEMENT DE L'ONTARIO AUX ARTS

LIBRARY AND ARCHIVES CANADA
CATALOGUING IN PUBLICATION

Alexis, André, 1957-, author
A / André Alexis.

ISBN 978-1-927040-79-9 (pbk.)

I. Title.

PS8551.L474A61 2013   C813'.54   C2013-903834-5

PRINTED IN CANADA

For Roo & Kim

Then things become all at once strange.
 – Margaret Laurence, *The Diviners*

There was once a book reviewer named Alexander Baddeley. Though he thought, as reviewers often do, that reviews were meant to be "corrosive" in order to be true, he was too much the lover of words to be cruel or condescending, dismissive or unkind.

To make up for his "failings," Baddeley sometimes flaunted his own (wilfully acquired) quirks as if they were the marks of deep feeling. For instance, he inevitably ate a single Brussels sprout and vanilla yoghurt for lunch, and he refused to take the subway because he was "afraid of snakes." (He was afraid of neither snakes nor subways.) None of this helped his reputation, though. Among the very few who cared about book reviews, Baddeley was known for his bland diction and his so-so mind. In a word, he was unsuccessful.

Still, at the heart of the man, there was a longing to be better — to be more acute, deeper, more understanding — and this almost palpable longing made his company desirable to others. It inspired sympathy and a certain amount of pity as well. Among those who pitied him was the book editor of the *Globe and Mail*, Leo Martinson, a man who, once a month, assigned Baddeley a book to review, thus assuring him of the $300 that were the basis of his income. To earn the money he needed for food – because his rent in Cabbagetown was $300 a month – Baddeley reviewed other books elsewhere and sold his review copies to second-hand book shops as soon as he had done with them. In this way, he made a miniscule living, eating little, and going nowhere that cost money.

As concerns Baddeley's sensibility, there is one more thing to say, but it is the most important thing. Alexander Baddeley would not sell the books of Avery Andrews. These he kept in a squat, glass-fronted, bookcase in his room at the boarding house. The seven books of poetry Avery Andrews had written shared space with a *King James Bible*, a complete Shakespeare, a *Strunk & White*, a Roget's, and a concise Oxford Dictionary. These books were Baddeley's valuables, held behind shatterproof glass, secured to his desk, locked against the vagrants who, from time to time, wandered in off the street and ransacked the rooms of the house where Baddeley lived.

The books of Avery Andrews – *First, After First, More, Again More, Still More, More Two* and *More Three* – were, despite their bewilderingly mundane titles, treasured in those circles where poetry had any standing at all. Even among Andrews' most fervent admirers, however, Baddeley was exceptional. He had memorized every one of the 500 poems Andrews had published. He knew those that were considered "canonical" as well as those that were merely brilliant. Baddeley's love for Andrews' verse was an un-dimmable light in his soul and he would have done anything to meet the poet.

In his desire to meet Avery Andrews, Baddeley was not alone. No one had seen Andrews in a long time. Few could remember him, save for one of his high school classmates who did not so much remember Andrews as he did the blank in his memory where, at some point, Andrews must have been: Avery sitting beside him in class; Avery drinking from a water fountain; Avery winning an award for physics. Whatever the reason for his withdrawal from society, Avery Andrews had not allowed a photograph of himself to be taken in decades, had not granted an interview, had not collected any of the awards his poetry had won.

Andrews' "hauteur" appealed to most of his readers. To them, it seemed fitting that the writer of almost glacially perfect work should live beyond the world, inaccessible. Andrews' attitude was particularly appealing to Baddeley. It was "superb" in a way Baddeley imagined himself emulating if he had *half* of Andrews' talent. He revered Andrews' silence but, like all fervent admirers, there was something behind the reverence. There was the conviction that, should they ever meet, he and Andrews would understand each other.

Also: Baddeley was working on what he hoped would be a magnum opus, a critical study entitled *Time and Mr. Andrews: Chronos in the Poetry of Avery Andrews.* (The title alone had cost him a few white nights. He had agonized over its every word and diacritical mark.) Yes, Baddeley wanted Andrew's approval, but even better would be Andrews' involvement, an interview, say, something to let his admirer know that *Time and Mr Andrews* was not wrong-headed.

Unfortunately, Baddeley had no idea how to go about contacting the poet. Andrews' publisher refused to pass on the least scrap of correspondence. Nor were they impressed by Baddeley's credentials as a reviewer. It did not seem to trouble them that they were denying Andrews access to a careful and committed reader. Without the help of Andrews' publisher, contacting the poet seemed unlikely.

The key to finding Avery Andrews was nearer to hand than Baddeley imagined, however. It was in the person of his friend, Gilbert "Gil" Davidoff. Davidoff, a mediocre novelist who thought highly of himself, was a compulsive womanizer. Among the women who'd given herself to him (in the misplaced hope that the intensity of his self-love might be matched by his love for another) there was one, a certain Marva Wilson, who'd had a relationship with Avery Andrews. It was a relationship of which she was shyly proud, being herself an admirer of poetry.

This information had come to Davidoff in an unexpected way. He had finished with Marva Wilson. After fucking, he had thanked her, as if their lovemaking had been a sort of cordiality, like opening a door for someone at a mall. Reaching for his shoes and socks, he'd turned to catch the small, compact woman looking at him.

– You know the story, Davidoff had said. Rambling man. Got to keep moving.

– You're not even that good a writer, said Marva bitterly.

– Right, said Davidoff. And who'd you say your father was? Northrop Frye?

– How can you be so cruel? she asked. What did I ever do to you?

– Now this, said Davidoff to Baddeley some time later, was the moment of truth. Two choices. You either run or you stay and smooth things over. But I like to smooth things over, 'cause if your reputation's in tatters you don't get what matters. You know what I mean? I'm sure you've been in the same position.

As a point of fact, Alexander Baddeley had never been in the same position, but he nodded sagely, inviting his friend to continue. There wasn't all that much to continue with, however. Davidoff had soothed Marva's feelings by pretending to care about her literary opinions. Then, just before she fell asleep, she'd let it slip that she had dated Avery Andrews, that they had been in love. Davidoff had – *for Baddeley's sake*, you understand – expressed admiration mixed with "just the right touch of incredulity." So, as she fell asleep, Marva had felt compelled to convince him. She had described the house on Cowan where he lived. And she had described the man himself: he was short; dark-haired but greying; his eyes small, his brow making them seem as if they were recessed; his mouth almost dainty; his skin smooth; his fingers long and elegant. And then there was the way he dressed. He invariably wore a yellow cardigan and oxblood oxfords. Winter, spring, summer and fall. A proper ritual: always the same sweater and shoes.

– A yellow cardigan and oxblood oxfords? asked Baddeley.

– I know, said Davidoff. No writer should wear a cardigan, unless he's dead.

Baddeley was too excited by what he'd heard to be offended by Davidoff's words. Imagine: Avery Andrews lived in Toronto.

All these years wondering where Andrews might be and he was in Baddeley's own city. And he lived in Parkdale! Now, that was an odd detail. Parkdale was nondescript, filled (in Baddeley's mind) with would-be artists and sad foreigners, with low-rent criminals and aspiring young professionals. Yet, what better place for a man who sought anonymity? It was just the neighbourhood for a genius like Andrews, when you really thought about it.

(Parkdale was on the other side of town from his rooming house, but it was still possible – perhaps even likely – that he had met Andrews on a street somewhere. No, on second thought, it was not likely. He could not have passed a man like Avery Andrews – a poet whose mind and spirit were indissociable from his (that is, Baddeley's) own soul – without recognizing him at once.)

Then again, had Marva Wilson been telling the truth or had she been saying any old thing in order to impress Gil? That was the question and, when asked, Gil could not say for certain. Marva had sounded sincere, he'd said. But, then, Gil Davidoff did not believe that any woman to whom he'd made love could be insincere, acute sexual gratitude being very like sodium pentothal. Baddeley was skeptical about the "truth-telling" that happens after lovemaking. He himself had managed to lie while talking to women with whom he'd just copulated. Actually, he had not lied. He had, once or twice, avoided speaking the truth in order to spare his lover's feelings. But the point still stood: Why should a woman not be able to fabricate or stretch a truth in similar circumstances? Worse yet, a host of mitigations occurred to him: Marva was telling the truth about some aspects of her story (the cardigan, say) but not others; Marva was telling the truth but Andrews had moved from Parkdale; Marva was lying but knew the truth; Marva had been the victim of a man claiming to be Avery Andrews ...

Still, thanks to Gil Davidoff, Baddeley had been given a hint, a provocation, somewhere to look or, if Marva proved unreliable, somewhere it was pointless to look.

Parkdale was a two-hour walk from Cabbagetown. (Baddeley could not afford the streetcar.) And though Cowan was not a long street, it was just long enough — almost a kilometre, running from south of Springhurst north to Queen Street — to be difficult for one man to patrol on his own. At which end of Cowan should he begin? Should he walk up and down the street looking for a man in a yellow cardigan? He — that is Baddeley – would almost certainly look suspicious. And what would he do if he actually found Avery Andrews? How would he address him? What would he say? How would Andrews react?

These were all questions to which Baddeley gave himself easy answers. Excited by even the faintest possibility of meeting Andrews, he refused to allow practical concerns to stand between himself and the poet. He would walk up and down Cowan. For one week, beginning at the furthest point south, he would walk the southernmost end of the street: Springhurst to

King. The following week, he would walk north between King and Queen. In the event he met a man in a cardigan and reddish oxfords, he would follow him about for a day, watching to see where the man went and to which address he returned. Once he'd found the man's house, he would — at some later time — break in and leave a copy of *Time and Mr. Andrews* somewhere prominent: on the kitchen counter, say, or on a living room table. How could Andrews — if it was Andrews — be anything but intrigued by such an intrusion? More: once Andrews had read the manuscript, he would — wouldn't he? — welcome Baddeley's company. (And if the man he found was not Andrews? Well, that would be unfortunate, it's true, but there were worse things in life — weren't there? — than a home invader who stole nothing but left a manuscript behind.)

Baddeley set out in search of Andrews the day after learning about Marva. He was immediately rewarded. At eleven o'clock on his first morning patrolling Cowan, Baddeley saw a man in reddish oxfords leaving the house at number 29. To be more expansive ... it was a cool but sunny day in November. Beyond the highway and the asphalt promenade, the lake was greenish-grey and as placid as a corpse. Baddeley was filled with the spirit of adventure. He was so excited at the thought of meeting Avery Andrews that he did not immediately clock the man coming out of number 29. Of course, but for his oxblood shoes the man was the essence of nondescript.

– That couldn't be him

was Baddeley's first thought. But then, as if to mock Baddeley's disbelief, the man turned towards him, unbuttoned the dark raincoat he was — oddly, given the sunshine — wearing, and revealed the canary yellow cardigan he had on beneath it. The man slid the key to his front door into the pocket of his sweater and then set off along Cowan, heading north.

Immediately, despite the sunshine, it began to rain.

Though he did not (*could* not) believe that the man walking before him was any kind of poet, Baddeley chose to follow him rather than dawdling in the rain waiting for a more likely candidate. Also, he assumed that pursuit would keep him warm. How true this turned out to be! The man walked quickly, so that it was difficult for Baddeley to keep up. Then, instead of waiting for a streetcar at King the man kept going: from King to Bathurst, and along Bathurst north to Dundas. It was a walk of some four kilometres that left Baddeley out of breath but unchilled.

Though Baddeley managed to keep up with the stranger, the man finally shook him in the most unusual way. That is, though the stranger seemed entirely unaware that he was being followed, Baddeley lost him in the basement of the Toronto Western Hospital. As quickly as one can say "gone", the man disappeared. No, it was more mysterious than that. The man took the stairs down. Baddeley followed. The man stepped into a room: Radiography 11A. Baddeley hesitated. What would he say, once inside? How would he justify his intrusion? He stared at the grey door, its shiny metal panel. And after a minute, he hit on the most obvious excuse. He would pretend to have lost his way. Once inside, he would take a close look at the man in the cardigan, then he would apologize and leave.

Baddeley had the words

– I'm so sorry

on the tip of his tongue as he pushed the door open. In fact, he said those very words to the empty room.

The room was thirty feet by thirty feet by thirty feet. Its ceiling lights — far above — were banks of fluorescents tubes. It had one door, only one, the one by which Baddeley had entered. There was, in other words, no obvious way for the short man to have left. Not only was the room empty of occupants, but it was also bereft of furniture or any sort of medical equipment. It being a room in radiography, one might have expected a side chamber or alcove in which the controls for an X-ray generator were kept. There was no such alcove, only the empty, white cube.

More peculiar still: the room was not quite empty. Yes, Baddeley was alone, but there seemed to be another world in there with him. As if the room were the aperture of a conch shell, he heard the sound of the sea and, along with it, the tones of familiar voices. The voices belonged to his parents, both of whom were long dead. The effect of hearing his parents' voices was deeply disturbing and Baddeley left the room at once.

Once outside of 11A, the world was restored to him. He knew exactly where he was: the basement of Toronto Western Hospital. He stood before a door on which the word "Radiography" was stencilled. In fact, the "real" world came back to him with such force that he felt puzzled rather than alarmed at what he'd experienced. The man in the cardigan had eluded him. No doubt about it. And the voices he'd heard? Nothing more than the hum of fluorescence. His imagination had played tricks on him. He was sure of it.

He was less certain about how to proceed. Should he leave a copy of his manuscript in the living room at 29 Cowan? He wasn't convinced the short man actually *was* Avery Andrews, but one had to start somewhere. Why not start at the home of this gentleman who, after all, had both the yellow cardigan and the oxblood shoes?

He hadn't worked out how he would break into the man's house but, as it happened, this was no problem at all. Though the man in the cardigan had locked his front door, the back door was open. So, Baddeley walked into a spotless kitchen. At least, "spotless" is what he thought on entering. But it was more that the place seemed uninhabited, expectant. There were no cobwebs and not much dust. The rooms were in order, the furniture arranged "just so." The lamps and wicker wastebaskets, the books in bookcases and the pictures on the walls were all neatly arranged. The place smelled faintly of incense. The further he went into the house, the less likely it seemed that anyone actually lived there.

Despite his sense that something wasn't right, Baddeley placed a copy of his manuscript — which he'd optimistically brought with him — on a coffee table in the living room. He left the house by the door he'd come in, resolving to return the following morning. But as Baddeley closed the kitchen door behind him and turned to go, he was confronted by the man in the yellow cardigan.

Caught off guard, Baddeley stuttered.

– I'm sorry. I'm sorry, he said. The door was open. I thought there was someone home.

The man stared at Baddeley a moment.

– I'm home now, he said.

– That's just it, said Baddeley. I thought a friend of mine

lived here. That's why I went in. I must have the wrong address.

– Stop lying, said the man. I'm Avery Andrews and I know who you are, assassin.

When he thought about this moment later — and he was to think about it often — Baddeley thought about how strange his face must have looked. On learning that he had found Avery Andrews, the emotions that coursed through him were myriad, contradictory, and sharply experienced. He felt excitement, wonder, fear, confusion, guilt, deference, arrogance, and disbelief. And each emotion must have imposed its own fleeting expression on his face.

– But, but, but …, he said.

Andrews interrupted him.

– I apologize, he said. I shouldn't have called you "assassin." Let's play this out.

– Play what out?

was Baddeley's first thought, but he almost dutifully followed Andrews back into the house. They walked through the kitchen into the living room.

– Don't sit down, said Andrews. I don't like housecleaning.

Baddeley stood, as Andrews sat down on the sofa. Andrews saw Baddeley's manuscript, picked it up from the coffee table — Baddeley's heart raced as his idol touched its pages — and threw it so that *Time and Mr. Andrews* hit Baddeley on the shoulder.

– You don't know anything about my work, said Andrews. None of you do. You're all deluded.

The bitterness in Andrews' voice was so corrosive, Baddeley accepted his own insignificance as if it were an obvious fact.

– Yes, he said. But if only you'd help me interpret your work, it would be even more popular than it is.

– Are you out of your mind? asked Andrews. I write poetry. It's not meant to be popular. Anyway, I can't help you interpret what I don't understand myself.

It was not going as Baddeley had hoped. He was certain a mind as acute as Andrews' would know the springs and coils of its own mechanism intimately. If only he could coax certain things from the poet.

– Mr. Andrews, Baddeley said, I really believe people would have a deeper appreciation for your work if …

Andrews cut him off.

– You don't understand, he said. I can't help you. I know nothing about my poems. I don't understand them at all. The only thing I know for certain is where they come from. I'll share that with you. That's what you want, isn't it?

On hearing Andrews' words, it was – for Baddeley – as if a distant star had entered the living room. Did he want to know the source of Andrews' poetry? Yes, he most certainly did.

– Thank you, Mr. Andrews. You don't know how much it would mean if you helped me understand where the poems come from.

For the first time, Avery Andrews smiled.

– They come from God, he said.

– Oh …, said Baddeley. They come from God.

He did not hide his disappointment.

– I believe it's God, said Andrews. But I've never asked. I've been too busy taking things down. You can decide for yourself.

It would have been difficult for Baddeley to say which aspect of this moment shook him most. Was it the change in Andrews' tone, from bitter to ... something else? Or was it Andrews' strange offer to show him how the poems came "from God"? With creative types, there was always the possibility of madness, but Andrews' poetry had always seemed to Baddeley so sane and clear that the idea the poet himself was mad had not once — not in all the readings and re-readings — occurred to him.

Baddeley assumed Andrews would invite him to his desk, to the place where inspiration touched him and then lecture him about creativity. He did not imagine that Andrews would take him to see the "god" in question. But it appeared that's what Andrews intended to do. They walked to King and from there they took the streetcar.

– I prefer to walk, said Andrews. But I'm tired.

And he paid Baddeley's fare.

Where's this madman taking me? Baddeley wondered. But he went anyway. Avery Andrews was determined to show him *something* and Baddeley's love for Andrews' work was sufficient to spur him on. But how strange genius was! Like something from a world where they breathe iridium.

As they approached Bathurst, the Wheat Sheaf tavern looking gothic in the silvery afternoon, Andrews spoke.

– So, you want to be a poet, he said.

– I don't have the talent to be a poet, answered Baddeley. I only wish I could write the poetry you write. It would ...

Andrews cut him off.

– I wanted to be a *novelist*, he said. I've always hated poetry.

They got off the streetcar at Bathurst, and Baddeley, alert in the company of Avery Andrews, looked up at the world. In one distance, the city rose to a craggy peak of metal, cement, and glass. In another, it was the lake that seemed to rise, like the inside of a glinting, grey-green cup. Behind them was the Parkdale from which they'd come.

– We'll walk from here, said Andrews.

Which they did, going wordlessly north, until they came to the Western.

We're going to Radiography 11A, Baddeley thought, alarmed, but they went, rather, to the fifth floor of the north wing. As they left the elevator, Avery Andrews stood still a moment before moving towards Ward 55A.

Now, disappearance generally moves along a line from "done with mirrors" to "sudden drop." The *suddenness* of a disappearance is, of course, part of what makes it uncanny. And if, on entering the room, Avery Andrews had disappeared in any of the "usual" ways, Baddeley would have been dismayed and, no doubt, frightened. But as the two went into Ward 55A, Andrews was absorbed by the room. It was as if the man were a streak of ink blotted up, his disappearance taking a full five seconds: time enough for Baddeley to wonder what was happening; time enough for him to realize he was alone in the same room he had entered in the hospital's basement — thirty feet by thirty feet by thirty feet, white. More than that, it was now obvious to Baddeley that the room could not be as it appeared to be, its dimensions making it impossible to fit between the fourth and sixth floors of the Toronto Western.

As much as Baddeley feared the madness of others, he was even more terrified of losing his *own* sanity. At the "absorption" of Avery Andrews, he looked away, as if he'd inadvertently seen something taboo. No sooner did he look away, however, than

55A turned into a typical ward: a ceiling ten feet above them with four banks of fluorescent lights; four beds, all of them occupied; a window looking out on another wing of the hospital, beyond which he could see more buildings and smoke rising from a tall chimney.

Standing beside the patient in the bed furthest from the door was Avery Andrews. In the bed was a very old man or, perhaps, a young one with a long, white beard. It was difficult to "read" the patient, but something about the man did not feel old. Without moving his lips or at all shifting position, the whitebeard said

– Come closer.

It was as if a statue had spoken. There was no doubt that the "statue" had spoken to *him*, however. So, warily, and still shaken by his vision of Andrews' absorption by the impossible room, Baddeley approached.

– You're interested in poetry, said the patient.

Once again, the patient's lips did not move. It was both uncanny and fascinating.

– It is better if you don't look at me, said the patient. I am not where you see me, but I am close.

– Look out the window, said Andrews.

And Baddeley noticed that Avery Andrews had turned away from the patient, had all the while been observing the smoke as it writhed from the chimney — bringing to Baddeley's mind a thin, old woman struggling out of a stone boot. The world could not be as he was now experiencing it and still be the world. Therefore, he had lost his mind, or some drug — mysteriously administered — had taken it from him.

The patient said

– It wouldn't make any difference if you *did* lose your mind.

Alexander Baddeley felt light-headed. The room spun 290 degrees and the floor politely rose to meet him. What met him first, however, was the laughter of the patient — the last sound he heard before he lost consciousness. No, that's too easily said: "he lost consciousness." As if something were taken away. In this instance, it would be truer to say that Alexander Baddeley *gained* a consciousness that, manifestly, was not his own. He fell to the floor, but instead of darkness there came … not voices, exactly, but a presence, something like the soundless manifestation of a collective. There on the floor with him, a knot of red ants were at work carrying off the remnants of a crust of bread, and it seemed to Baddeley that he would have given anything to be one of them. That is, he experienced the purposeful delicacy of "mindlessness."

How long he spent both inside *and* beside himself, Baddeley never learned. After a time, he woke in Andrews' house on Cowan. Judging by the light coming through the windows, hours or perhaps minutes had passed. There was sunlight but, for some reason, Baddeley imagined it was evening. He was on the living room sofa. Andrews was standing above him.

– What happened? Baddeley asked.

Avery Andrews looked down at him, all sympathy.

– Don't look at Him, he said. And try not to speak. Look out the window or keep your eyes closed. There's nothing to see, anyway.

– But what happened?

– You've been out for a while. I didn't know where you'd gone. I found you here, because He told me you'd be here. It could have been worse. I was gone for three days the first time He spoke to me. But don't think about that. You want to write, don't you?

At that moment, Baddeley had no idea what he wanted and no clear idea how he felt. He was concerned for his state of mind. Had he really met "God"? Or was it, rather, that Andrews had found some way to pull him into a delusion? (What, if it came to that, did "God" mean, in this situation?) Yet, along with the fear and the mistrust, there was exhilaration. Baddeley was in thrall to the depth of feeling he'd experienced while watching the red ants carry crumbs away. If he was capable of feeling anything so deeply — and it was a revelation to him that he *was* capable — it might just be possible for him to write poetry as well, especially if Avery Andrews was guiding him. Insane though the man might be, Baddeley would follow him quite a ways, if it led to such depths.

– Yes, he said. I want to learn to write like you.

Andrews said

– It'll be a short apprenticeship. There isn't much to learn. You have to prepare yourself, that's all. I'll show you how you do it, then you'll take over from me. If I were you, I'd get my life in order. Pay off your debts. Say goodbye to your friends. Three days from now, meet me at the Western at seven a.m. If you find the room on your own, everything I have will be yours. This house, that sofa you're lying on. Everything.

Andrews held up his hand, as if to ward off conversation.

– Three days, he said. I'll answer the rest of your questions then. Now, please ... I need to get ready.

Although, at that moment, there were a thousand questions

on Baddeley's mind, when Andrews asked him to leave, he got up from the sofa and left the house, still in shock. Nor, in the days that followed, could Baddeley grasp why it was important that he "get his life in order." Neither why nor *how*, for that matter. His life amounted to so little, it was, in a sense, inevitably "in order."

He did follow one bit of Andrews' advice, though. He spoke with a friend. The day before he was to meet the poet, Baddeley met Gil Davidoff at *The Cobourg*, a bar in Cabbagetown. More than anything, he wanted to tell *someone* about his encounters with Avery Andrews. Davidoff would not give a damn about his experiences and Baddeley knew it. That was why he wanted to tell Davidoff everything. Davidoff's self-regard had a way of turning even the most dire things in Baddeley's life trivial, rendering them less painful.

They were sitting at the front of *The Cobourg*. Their table was in a bay, its tall windows looking out onto Parliament Street. Cabbagetown was not bustling, exactly, but it was *almost* lively.

– I met Avery Andrews, Baddeley said.

– You see? answered Davidoff. I told you chicks can't lie to me.

– You're right, said Baddeley. And he wants me to meet him at the Toronto Western tomorrow morning. He didn't say where.

– The Western's not that big, said Davidoff. I met a couple nurses there once. They're pretty good, nurses. Know their stuff. But I prefer actresses. You can screw an actress for weeks without doing the same woman twice. Know what I mean?

– Not really ..., said Baddeley. But what about Andrews? Do

you think I should go? I felt like I was hallucinating when I was with him. I really think he might be crazy.

– So? You should meet him if you want to, said Davidoff. What's the worst a poet can do? Throw up on your shoes? Just remember, Hemingway punched Stevens' lights out. Not the other way 'round. And that's how poets *should* be treated.

Davidoff turned away to look out at the late-autumn world, lowered his dark-rimmed glasses to get a better look at a woman just then passing on the street.

– You think I should go, then, said Baddeley.

– What? Sure. Are we *still* talking about you? answered Davidoff.

– No, no, said Baddeley. I'll figure it out.

So, despite his trepidation, he went to the hospital on the appointed day, at seven in the morning. Having no idea where in the maze of Toronto Western he was to meet Avery Andrews, he simply followed what might be called "instinct." It was not a strong "instinct." He wandered about for an hour before he went up to the sixth floor of the east wing. He felt a certain "curiosity" about a janitor's closet between two wards. The closet was unnumbered. A panel on the door said "Employees Only." When Baddeley opened the door, however, he found himself in the ward in which he had first encountered the patient, and there the patient was again. Avery Andrews stood near his "God," looking out the windows.

The room was, of course, astonishing. It could not possibly fit in the closet Baddeley had entered. What's more, this time, the view from the windows was as if from the middle of Lake Ontario looking back on Toronto, looking back, impossibly, on the Toronto Western and on the very window in which Baddeley and Andrews were framed. Looking out the window and raising his right hand, Baddeley saw his own hand rising in the distance. It was, to say the least, disconcerting: an illusion of some sort, obviously, but most confusing.

Without waiting for a question, the patient said

– The answers I could give you would not help. I am here because I too suffer. You remember how peaceful it was for you to share the mind of ants at work? So it is for me when I am in your mind, my son. It is such bliss to find simplicity.

It didn't seem to Baddeley that his thoughts were simple.

– Your thoughts *are* simple, said the patient. You're only worried about what you call your sanity. A negligible matter, Alexander. The boundary is subtle, even for me. But, I understand you'd like to write poetry. There are two obstacles to your writing. One is within you. You must learn to listen to me when I am with you. And that will not always be pleasant. The other obstacle is before you. You'll have to free Mr Andrews, if you'd like to take his place. I don't believe you're capable of it, but Avery is convinced that you are.

Avery Andrews turned to face the man he had, from the moment he'd set eyes on him, assumed to be his killer: Alexander Baddeley.

– I *want* to die, he said.

Nothing about this moment made any sense to Baddeley. For one thing, who could comprehend the trajectory he was expected to make: from admirer of Avery Andrews to Andrews' assassin? How was he supposed to put aside years and years of admiration for Andrews? At this moment, in this place, for this audience, he was to murder a man he loved? There was no question of him doing any such thing. Whatever Andrews' emotional problems, Baddeley could not see himself killing a man who was one of the only sources of beauty and consolation in his life. Someone had misjudged him.

Turning towards the patient, Baddeley asked

– Who are you?

– Don't look at him, said Andrews. Look at me. I'm the one begging for mercy. I've been bound to him for thirty years. I've looked after him for thirty years. Every line of poetry I've written, everything you've admired has come from him, from listening to him. I'm nothing but a vessel for his ramblings. I want to be free. I *want* to die.

– But I'm not a killer, said Baddeley.

– You *must* be, said Andrews, or you wouldn't have found me.

Turning toward the patient but not looking at him directly, Andrews pleaded.

– Tell him, he said

– What should I tell him? asked God.

– Tell him that I'm nothing. There's no poetry in me, except for what you put there. All these years, he's admired a stenographer. It all comes from you. There's nothing of me in it. I'm a fraud. He could do what I do just as well as I do. Better! He's a critic!

His hands shaking, Andrews pulled a notebook and pen from his shirt pocket. Opening the book to a blank page, he held it up for Baddeley to see.

– Look, he said

and, then, turning to the hospital bed, he bowed his head and mumbled something or other. Baddeley could not make out Andrews' words. Baddeley himself was thinking of nothing so much as how to escape from the men into whose awful company he'd wandered – the poet and his "God." But then, a strange "mind" was made manifest to him. Yes, insofar as he could recognize "divinity," the mind Baddeley experienced was "divine." In a way, it was the twinned opposite of the red ants' mind. While *there*, with the ants, a purity beyond words had brought peace; here, in this presence, he experienced a peace brought forth from infinite ramification: mind without end, pattern without border, a reachable horizon. For the first time in his life, Alexander Baddeley knew a different order of beauty, an unworldly vision that lay just within the range of words.

How long this moment lasted, neither man could have said. It was accompanied only by the scritch-scratching of Andrews' pen on paper, by the shedding of words – a shedding that seemed to Baddeley more an irritation than a gift, though Baddeley had been, and knew he had been, attendant at the creation of a poem by Avery Andrews. The poem was unmistakably Andrews' but unfamiliar …

> *While the Eumenides sharpen their thumbs*
> *To scratch our prophecies, bitter in fall:*
> *The immortal benefits of glorious life,*
> *Resplendence of our everlasting story,*
> *No prayer advances down the shopping mall,*
> *Pure wheat of which is baked the bread of life.*

When the spell was broken, when the moment had passed, Baddeley and Andrews stood facing each other, exhilarated, both of them fascinated by the residue that God's presence had left: poetry, though these — oddly enough — were *not* the words Baddeley himself would have saved from the listening.

If there had been doubt about the patient's identity before this moment, there was no doubt left in Baddeley's mind immediately after it. The illusions, the tricks with time and space, were paltry compared to the vision he and Andrews had shared. Baddeley was ecstatic. Andrews' exhilaration was short-lived, however. He had been here before, often. He knew this moment well and was tired of it, though he tried to talk it up.

– You see? Said Andrews. It's wonderful, isn't it? How could you turn this down, Alexander? Think what it would mean to live your life in His presence!

Every one of Andrews' words rang hollow.

– All I'm asking, he continued, is this small thing. Please, Alexander. I'm being eaten alive by the sacred! No! I don't mean it that way. It's not as bad as that. It's wonderful. But I'd like to pass it on. For that, I need someone who'll free me.

– Why don't you free yourself? asked Baddeley.

– I can't. I have a duty to …

Andrews moved his head in the direction of the Being in the hospital bed. Neither man looked at Him directly, but as Andrews completed his ever-so-slight gesture there was a moment of desolation. God's recession was not gradual or graceful. It was not like a wave receding from the shore. It was immediate, as if all seas had suddenly ceased to be. There was, in Baddeley's soul, the most complete abandonment he had experienced; so agonizing that, for a moment, it occurred to him that his life was worthless, that the best thing for him, under the circumstances, was death. In fact, he looked towards the window wondering how high up they were.

But there was no window. There was no window, no ward, no God, no beds, no lacustrine vista. He and Avery Andrews were in a darkened room that smelled of disinfectant. At least, he was in a darkened room of some sort. He could not see the person with him. Rather, he heard the muffled sobs of another man, the intake of breath. Baddeley reached out in the dark, meaning only to touch Andrews' shoulder, but as he did the door to the room opened and there was a flood of light.

– What the hell's wrong with you people? Can't you do your nasty business at home? This is a hospital, for Christ's sake!

Baddeley and Andrews were in a janitor's closet. Baddeley's hand was raised. It was in the vicinity of Andrews' cheek, as if the nurse who'd opened the door had interrupted them in mid caress. Both men stared at her as if she were an apparition.

– Come on, get out of there, the nurse said, or I'll call the guard.

Still dazed, Andrews and Baddeley left the closet, walking down the hall towards an elevator.

At the entrance to the hospital, Andrews — who had kept quiet and avoided Baddeley's gaze — suddenly held on to Baddeley's arm, keeping him from leaving the premises, the sliding doors opening and closing, closing and opening, like Scylla and Charybdis.

– Please, said Andrews.

And he tried to convince Baddeley that, despite the desolation one felt when God turned his back (a thing that happened after every poem), the chance to be His servant was worth all. Wasn't it better to be *Abd Allah* than a second-rate reviewer? Wasn't it worth the personal sacrifice to attain the heights of Art? And why would he — that is, Baddeley — have gone through such trouble to find him — that is, Andrews — if, in the depths of his soul, he wasn't searching for this very servitude. Yes, it would be inconvenient to do away with Andrews. But Andrews wanted nothing more than release.

– You'd be doing me a kindness, he said. I'll even take poison, if you administer it.

For Baddeley, this was a complex moment made even more bewildering by its proximity to the sublime episode he had just lived. It isn't every day, after all, that one meets "God." Although, in light of the fact that this "god" seemed to approve of murder, doubt about the Being's true nature had already begun to dampen Baddeley's enthusiasm. Yet, there was enthusiasm still. How could a man who had for so long studied the *ends* of creativity (books and paintings and such) be anything but thrilled by his (admittedly strange) experience of creativity's origin? Some part of Baddeley's soul wanted to go on experiencing "inspiration" for ever and ever. But, really, he wanted to go on experiencing it as an *observer*. The strangeness of Andrews' attitude (Andrews' desire for death) frightened him, and he was afraid to be alone in the room with whatever that presence was.

Maybe, if Andrews had allowed him time to think about it, time to consider what it would be like to live *without* inspiration, time to long for the listening, Baddeley might have more seriously considered his plea for death. (Though, when he *did* think about it, later, it brought nightmares: pushing Andrews onto subways tracks, throwing him from a bridge or a tall building, stabbing him, shooting him, drowning him, his hands around the poet's neck, breaking it as one would a bread stick ...) Instead, feeling rushed and bewildered, Baddeley wanted only to get away from Avery Andrews. He wanted to get away from what Andrews had put him through and from the death Andrews wanted of him.

He pulled the poet's fingers from his arm and backed towards the sliding doors.

– Find someone else, he said. If you come near me again, I'll call the police.

– But you came to *me*, Andrews pleaded. You came to me!

Once out of the hospital, Baddeley looked to see if the man was following him. But, no, Avery Andrews stood rooted to his spot before the door, looking out at him as he looked back. So this was Avery Andrews: a forlorn, psychologically damaged man in reddish shoes. Once Baddeley was far enough away, once he was certain Andrews would not follow him, a sadness welled up to accompany his dismay. Andrews was pathetic, yes, but somewhere within Baddeley's soul the admiration he'd felt for Avery Andrews guttered but was not extinguished.

It had been a brief episode, nothing more than two (admittedly strange) days.

For as long as he was able, for months, Baddeley tried to suppress the memory, as one tries to suppress the memory of a woman one has loved and broken with in some humiliating way. And like the memory of a lost beloved, his encounters with Avery Andrews recurred to him at unexpected times, bringing confusion, anguish, and longing. Baddeley struggled to understand what had happened to him, and finally began to understand it in his own way. What had he done? He had sought out a poet whose work he'd long admired. He had found the man. And then? And then he had become the victim of an inexplicable and pointless hoax, brought to a ward in Toronto Western to interact with a life-sized puppet. After which, Andrews had pleaded for death.

There was neither sanctity nor mystery behind any of that. There was only a madness whose consequence was that Baddeley could no longer look at the books of Avery Andrews without a feeling of humiliation. (He did not, for all that, throw them out.)

A year passed — a year of fitful forgetting.

Although Baddeley sometimes managed to convince himself that he'd lived through a hoax, something inside of him had truly changed after the encounters at Toronto Western: his attitude, his sensibility, his understanding. *Something* had changed and deeply. His approach to literature — and so, to life — had shifted without him being conscious of the shifting. However false the apparition may have been, the experience of it had real consequences. Baddeley had participated in the creation of a poem. He had been only a few paces away from where lightning had struck and some of the charged particles had rearranged something in him.

This understanding — this *rearrangement* — influenced his reviews and, at the same time, poisoned reviewing for him. Even as he wrote his opinions — which were now perceptive, conscientious, and even, at times, brilliant — Baddeley knew his ability for what it was: trivial. The books he judged to be mediocre were not, objectively speaking, mediocre. They were "mediocre" because Baddeley could now clearly and resonantly reveal the particular angle (his own) from which they were "mediocre." That is, he could vividly express the fixity of his angle on things.

That this was all the ability any good reviewer has ever possessed did not console him.

Worse: as his reputation grew, as he was invited to write for better journals and papers, for American and British venues where a host of well-known critics plied their unvalued trade, he grew tired of his limitations. He grew weary, in other words, of his own perspective.

More: his disappointment deepened the chasm between himself and a world he'd once wished to inhabit — literary Toronto, with its endless book launches and poetry readings and literary festivals run by men whose only talent was, in essence, the ability to read. Here, the mid-listers trying desperately to keep afloat, networking, networking, networking; there, the poets just this side of insane nursing their childhood grudges. Here, the stars in the literary firmament (big teeth, pink palms, regal airs); there, the fresh-faced youth, trying their best not to seem overwhelmed or overjoyed or overawed. All their names began to lose sense: Onwood, Munwood, Mistwood ... Why, he wondered, had he ever wished to belong to such a cloud-cuckoo world?

Whereas, previously, he'd been kept from literary society by his envy and want of self-confidence, Baddeley was now driven from it by a certainty that the society of writers was almost infinitely less interesting than intercourse with books, books in which he could, at times, feel the presence he'd felt at the Toronto Western with Andrews. So, while the esteem in which he was held grew, his commerce with the world was impoverished. In fact, the signal moment in Baddeley's "year after the hospital" was the end of his friendship with Gil Davidoff.

Yes, Gil was self-absorbed and self-important but his flaws had never put Baddeley off. Speaking with Gil was like watching a bird with a broken wing attempt flight: round and round going nowhere. Davidoff could speak of nothing but himself for long and rarely strayed far from the subject. But Baddeley had always taken comfort in being led from his troubles by a mind that acknowledged no troubles but its own. Whenever he grew tired of himself, spending time with Davidoff allowed Baddeley to grow tired of someone else. It allowed him to return refreshed to his own company. He had enjoyed Gil's books for the same reason. They were not good but they were "Gil" and that had been enough.

As Baddeley's standing in the literary community grew, first Gil and then Gil's publisher, Lance Swann, asked him for a blurb for Gilbert "Gil" Davidoff's latest novel, *Slow Boat to Peru*. Baddeley agreed to do it, and if he had not read the book, if, rather, he had written a few words about how wonderful Gil's *company* had always been, all would no doubt have been fine between them. But Baddeley read the manuscript. It was, as Gil's novels always were, a pale, plainly written imitation of Malcolm Lowry: one man, heroically "drunk," absorbed by the detritus of his deliria. The only thing that ever changed, in Gil's fiction, was the locale. In the past, his protagonists — never more than stand-ins for Gil himself — had been delirious in Paris, delirious in Mexico, delirious in Bolivia, and delirious in Kuala Lumpur.

Baddeley's first thought on finishing his friend's book was that, the world having a nearly inexhaustible supply of place names, Gil's novel could be written over and over until cockroaches covered the face of earth. His second, and more charitable thought was that he would write, for friendship's sake, an anodyne blurb, something that could be taken for praise if it were left unexamined:

> I have read a marvellous book!
> — *Alexander Baddeley*

or

> Slow Boat to Peru is a real book!
> — *Alexander Baddeley*

or again

> Of all the books I have read, this one is by
> the wonderful Gil Davidoff!
> — *Alexander Baddeley*

But he found he could not write anything dishonest. Something in him was no longer biddable. And when Mr Swann asked him, more and more insistently as the publication deadline approached, for his blurb, Baddeley could only say that, this being the first time he had written a blurb for a friend's book, he was having difficulty finding words to express his feelings. This answer, delivered with a sigh and a tone of contrition, was enough for Mr. Swann. It was not enough for Gil himself, though. Gilbert "Gil" Davidoff was outraged that his friend, whom he now found he did not much like, could refuse so simple a request. Nor was he fooled by Baddeley's excuses.

Their breach came when the deadline passed and Baddeley had given Swann nothing. When next Baddeley saw Gil

Davidoff, Davidoff allowed him to gaze on his profile while he — that is, Gilbert "Gil" Davidoff — shed increasingly vituperative opinions about reviewers: reviewers in general; reviewers in Toronto; and reviewers who, without reason, thought too highly of themselves. Thereafter, Gilbert Davidoff could not be reached by Alexander Baddeley, no matter how Baddeley tried. And, at first, Baddeley did try. It was more as a matter of habit than anything else, though. Having made four or five calls, having left three or four messages on Gil's answering machine, it finally occurred to Baddeley that Gil Davidoff was petty, unworthy, and mean, that Davidoff was the literary scene and the literary scene was Davidoff. Disenchanted with one, why should he maintain his friendship with the other?

Another year passed.

Baddeley read books and wrote reviews. He was invited to be on panels devoted to this or that aspect of literature. His insights into the moment of the art work's conception and creation were particularly appreciated. He was commissioned to write longer essays on Pasternak, Avison, Cavafy, and Langston Hughes. He did not become wealthy but he was able to leave his rooming house for an apartment in the basement of 434 Runnymede. He could afford to take the streetcar when he wanted and there was talk of him writing a book about canadian literature.

All this should have been gratifying. The months should have passed quickly. But, if anything, time slowed. Baddeley became convinced that most of what passed for art was, in reality, an endless re-fashioning of the mire; endless recreations of the moments in the closet *after* God had forsaken him.

That dark moment in the closet, as well as the enthusiasm

that had preceded it, returned vividly to Baddeley with the publication of Avery Andrews' *Yet Again*. The fact of the publication was a shock to Baddeley. Avery Andrews had seemed on the verge of suicide. It was scarcely credible that he'd lived long enough to write another collection of poems. And yet, there was the proof, in the pages of the *Globe and Mail*: a review of Andrews' collection by Ismail Andersson who quoted from what he called one of the book's more remarkable poems, "The Eumenides," the very poem at whose inception Baddeley had been present:

> *While the Eumenides sharpen their thumbs*
> *To scratch on our windows prophecies, bitter crumbs —*
> *The immortal benefits of glorious life ...*

Reading those words, seeing them in the pages of the *Globe*, brought back the majesty at the heart of Andrew's work and they rekindled Baddeley's desire to write poetry himself. Baddeley was suddenly convinced that he knew the way to the place Andrews had been and so, along with his reviews, he began to write poetry.

Weeks after he began writing poetry, he stopped.

Not only was poetry difficult to accomplish but, for Baddeley, it was almost impossible even to begin. He had imagined that any word he put down would call out to the other words the poem needed. This was the opposite of what happened. Any word he wrote seemed almost to eradicate the rest of the English language. After three weeks, his "poems" consisted of abandoned stanzas and the occasional phrase, the most coherent of which was

I scale the glacier of your frozen eyes

a line that sounded wonderful as he wrote it, though, when he saw it the following day, he knew it for the doggerel it was.

And so, for the first time, Baddeley had a deeper sense of what it was he'd lost when he had turned Avery Andrews down: certainty, the knowledge that one's work was good. Two years on, he did not believe that Andrews had a link to God. Nor did he believe that by killing Andrews he would inherit some privileged relation to the poetic. What Baddeley now believed was that he might have learned from Andrews' derangement as, say, Jacques Prevel had learned at the feet of Antonin Artaud or as Anatoly Naiman had at those of Anna Akhmatova. He had been hasty to turn away from the poet's gift, however poisoned the gift might be. The memory of Andrews standing (forlorn) at the entrance to the Toronto Western returned to Baddeley with full, melancholy force.

More than that: after reading Andrews' latest collection, it seemed to Baddeley that Andrews had overcome the mental instability that had had him in its grip. The poems in *Yet Again* were of a lucidity that suggested peace of mind and acceptance of the world. And having agreed — having agreed with himself, in effect — that Andrews was almost certainly sane, Baddeley decided it would not be wrong to contact the poet again.

It was again November. Parkdale was grey, but it was a soft grey. Its streets were wet; its pedestrians in half-unbuttoned coats. The house at 29 was unchanged but, at the sight of it,

46

Baddeley felt as if he were walking into a recurring dream. He knocked on the door and rang the bell. He heard a woman's voice, faint and muffled, and then the door was opened as far as the bolted chain would allow. An Asian woman was on the other side: angular face, an ear sticking out from the black curtain that was her hair.

– I'm looking for Mr. Andrews, said Baddeley.

– He not heah, said the woman.

– Can you tell me where I could find him?

– He at hospital.

– At the Toronto Western?

– He at hospital.

The woman looked at him and he looked at her.

– Thank you, he said.

This little scene was repeated half a dozen times over the weeks that followed. Baddeley would knock – early in the morning, mostly, hoping to catch Andrews before he set off to find "inspiration." The door would be partially opened, and he would be told that Mr. Andrews was "at hospital." He would then go to the Toronto Western and wander the halls looking for Andrews.

Baddeley expected that, at some point, he would knock at the door and find Andrews at home. He was prepared to be patient. But as it happened, the next time he saw Avery Andrews Baddeley did not recognize the man. Andrews recognized *him*.

It was the evening of November 22nd and Baddeley was at the Toronto Western. He had walked about the wards with diminishing conviction. He'd been buttonholed by a number of insistently helpful nurses and he was on his way out when, as he passed through a waiting room, a man in a wheelchair caught his attention, held eye contact then signalled to him with the wave of a hand.

The man was bald, the freckles on his head "fresh", as if splattered from a pen with beige ink. He was almost swallowed by his blue-striped pyjamas and, incongruously, a yellow cardigan. It was the cardigan, of course, that jogged something in Baddeley's memory, so that he was thinking of Avery Andrews before he actually recognized the man. Andrews was unhealthily thin, cadaverous. His fingers were still elegant but the skin on his hand was almost translucent, the veins along the back of his hands a vivid blue. His eyes, which had always seemed recessed, now glimmered as though they were shining at the end of a dark tunnel.

Yes, this was Avery Andrews and, in a word, the man looked to be on his last legs.

– How strange to see you, Andrews said
or, rather, Andrews *managed* to say. No sooner were the words out than he began to cough, grimacing at each shudder of his chest, struggling to quell his body's insubordination.

– How strange, he said again. I didn't think you'd come. Please forgive me for how I behaved. I wasn't myself.

Again Andrews began to cough. A nurse approached them.

– Everything all right? she asked.

– Yes, said Andrews. This is my friend.

– Friend or not, said the nurse, I think it's time you were back in your room.

Andrews held on to Baddeley's wrist. His grip was not strong. The nurse said

– It isn't good for you to get excited, Mr. Andrews, but visiting hours are still on. You can go on talking in your room.

It was distressing to watch Avery Andrews as he was helped into his hospital bed. His limbs looked as though they might snap under the slightest pressure. It hurt to watch him stand up. (His body was so wasted it was easily supported by the sticks that were his legs.) More distressing still was the ginger hair on the back of his legs. Baddeley turned away until Andrews was tucked under the sheets and the nurse had asked if he wanted morphine and then, having inserted the drip, went off to other beds.

– I don't have much time, said Andrews. I want to tell you something, before the morphine kicks in. I was like you, but not like you. When I went to see Margaret Laurence, she recognized me immediately. And she knew what I was. I loved fiction more than I loved people. I still do. When I pushed her from the ferry, it was because she *wanted* to die and because I knew her art would live on in me. I see, now, that you don't love the art deeply enough, Alexander. You're too attached to me personally. I should have known, when you left that manuscript in my living room.

– Did you read it? asked Baddeley.

– I read as much of it as I could, son. You have everything wrong. You made me sound deep and heroic, but I'm none of the things you admire. I'm nothing. What you really admire is the Master's voice. For years, it's all I wanted to hear, too, but now I've had enough. I wanted you to end my servitude, like I ended Margaret's. I should have gotten to know you first. But I suppose things have worked out as they were meant to.

– What do you mean? asked Baddeley.

– You'll seek Him out, now, won't you?

– I don't think so, said Baddeley. I was looking for you.

Andrews grew visibly upset, but the morphine had begun to work and it was as if his emotions were passing through a kind of screen.

– You must look for him, Andrews said. You must. I can't leave until I know you will. He appears to any number of artists, but *this* identity of His is unique. This line is ... our line is ...

Anxious to calm the poor man, Baddeley said

– All right. I'll look for him. I promise.

– But the thing to remember, said Andrews, the thing is ... He's not always Himself. After all these years, I think I'm entitled to say that. There have been times when I'm *certain* God is not sane. He says there's no difference between sane and insane, but there is. You'll feel the difference, and you'll have to forgive Him. I don't think He can help Himself.

– I'm sorry, said Baddeley. But I don't know what you're talking about.

– You'll see things you don't want to see. He can't help it. Forgive Him or you'll end up as unhappy as I was. As we've all been. Listen, I sold the house. I'm sorry. I thought you were gone for good. You'll need somewhere to live ...

Andrews was now visibly too drug-clouded to go on talking. He could not keep his eyes open. He had spent all his energy on their conversation.

– Come back tomorrow, he managed.

He then grasped at Baddeley's arm, some important thing on his mind.

– I know …, he said. I know …

But he could not finish his thought. He fell back onto the bed, mumbling.

As Baddeley looked down at Andrews' face, it occurred to him that, at the best of times, his relations with other people were tricky. Even so, this bond with Avery Andrews was baffling. He had sought Andrews out. He had discovered an unstable man. And now, the man was dying. Why should it be *his* duty to watch the gyroscope fall?

And yet, Baddeley felt compelled to return. He was fascinated by the spectacle of Andrews' death, saddened that (so it seemed) he alone would be with Andrews in this most private of moments. As well, he felt a certain pride that *he* should have been chosen to be with Andrews at the end. The encounter would almost certainly inform the next draft of *Time and Mr. Andrews*, a book he swore he would finish, despite Andrews' disappointing words.

The following morning, however, all was changed. At the reception desk, Baddeley was told that "Mr. Andrews" had died during the night. He had died peacefully, "in his sleep."

– I see, said Baddeley. Thank you.

The nurse, struck that her words had been taken with such equanimity, said

– Would you like to see the body? I don't think it's been taken from the room yet.

Not knowing what else to say under the circumstances and feeling that the nurse was doing her best to grant him some sort of favour, Baddeley said "thank you" and was directed to room 88A, the room in which he'd last seen Andrews alive.

It would be difficult to exaggerate Baddeley's confusion as he entered 88A. Without transition or warning, he found himself in the ward of Avery Andrews' god. The windows looked back from Lake Ontario at the room in which Baddeley now stood. The perspective made him ill. There were four beds in the room. In each of the beds was what looked to be a brilliant approximation of the human: flesh tones perfect, the postures natural, the eyes glinting as if moistened by tear ducts. But the mannequins — there's no other word for them — were all unmoving. One of them was in the image of Avery Andrews, another looked like Lucius Annaeus Seneca, and a third resembled Saint Teresa as Bernini had fashioned her: ecstatic.

Baddeley heard the word

– Welcome.

It came from the *fourth* mannequin, the one closest to the window. It "came from" the mannequin in the way a ventriloquist's voice "comes from" a dummy. The voice was in Baddeley's mind and his attention was somehow drawn to the mannequin nearest the window.

– Don't look at me for too long, said the voice. It's best if you look at the floor.

More to himself than not, Baddeley said

– All this is impossible. I must be dreaming.

– Since you don't know where you are, how can it matter if you're awake?

– It matters to *me*, said Baddeley. I don't want to be insane.

– I understand, said the voice. And I sympathize.

And God entered Baddeley's consciousness. Time stood still. The room broke the bounds of the building that held it, expanding to encompass all that Baddeley knew of the world. In an instant, he was "beside himself," he and his world detached from each other and, alienated, he was filled with the exhilaration that accompanies new or unexpected views. (Baddeley assumed the vantage was God-given or god-like or god-angled. On this occasion, what he experienced was too bright and glorious to be anything but divine.)

While he was inhabited by the sacred — if "sacred" is what it was — Baddeley knew what he wanted to say. That is, he knew what he wanted to *write*. Words tumbled from him in paragraphs; a novel came to being within his imagination. Along with the ecstasy of suddenly knowing the words he needed, however, there was an anxiety that he might not manage to keep *these* words, to remember them when it came time to write them down. So that, at the moment of deepest inspiration, Baddeley also felt anguish at the thought of how much he might lose.

Moments, minutes, hours after the Lord had taken him over, His presence withdrew. It did not vanish entirely but, all the same, the withdrawal brought agony.

– Stay, Baddeley pleaded.

– I cannot, said the Lord.

And He withdrew as time returned and the room retreated into itself, its only bed occupied by the remains of Avery Andrews; the only living presence that of Alexander Baddeley himself.

On first encountering this "being," Baddeley had assumed it was an aspect of Andrews' madness — a delusion so powerful it could be parcelled and shared. After this communion, he understood why Andrews had come to think it was sacred.

What he could not see was how Andrews had thought of the spirit as in any way "insane." Nothing that could lead a man to such heights could be considered anything but miraculous. Literally miraculous, as far as Baddeley was concerned. He had been mired in a longing to express himself. He had not managed a single good line of poetry. But after this moment in the hospital he was charged with words. Having paid his final respects to Avery Andrews, Baddeley returned to his apartment on Runnymede and began writing. For five days he worked without eating, stopping only for water, coffee or the Allen's apple juice he had in his fridge. He wrote the first chapters of a novel called *Home is the Parakeet*, a novel that existed fully formed in his imagination or, rather, *half*-formed like one of the statues left unfinished by Michelangelo, so that, for Baddeley, all was there. It was now only a matter of helping the thing from its integument.

(*Home is the Parakeet's* macabre first paragraph ...

The black-garbed soldiers, perhaps thirty in all, were preparing for a final assault on what was left of the village: two farms housing three dozen women and children, who were equipped with a couple of hunting rifles and almost no ammunition. One soldier guided a muzzled alligator on a leash. Several others heated their bayonets with acetylene torches. They formed a merry bunch, laughing as they set off.

is now, of course, among the best known passages of Canadian prose.)

And yet, when the first chapters were written, Baddeley

was uncertain about how to go on. He was overwhelmed by the number of roads his novel could take. Worse, it no longer seemed to him that his novel meant any *one* thing. No, his narrative of a man who returns from the Second World War traumatized at having witnessed the slaughter for food of exotic birds in a bird sanctuary now meant innumerable things. In his mind, *Home is the Parakeet* was a metaphor for everything from the struggle between man and nature to the nightmare of colonialism.

He went back to the Western.

This visit was much like the previous. Though God was not in 88A, Baddeley found the right room easily. Using only an instinct he did not know he possessed, he pushed open a door in the prenatal ward and found himself in what he now thought of as the "customary" place. And God — or whatever it was — overtook him at once. At once he was in the presence of God's vision which was also, for a time, his own: like a single image printed on two transparencies that are then overlaid, one atop the other. And when his time with "God" ended, Baddeley was both exhausted *and* wide awake.

(An unexpected gift: at times like this — after an encounter with "God" — he found himself susceptible to the city. Walking home from the hospital, the city seemed to have awakened *with* him. It was like dawn in the arms of someone he loved. It wasn't just a matter of the usual attractions: the lake, its beaches, the quiet of Mount Pleasant. No, in these moods, Baddeley loved every aspect of Toronto: the light of day, the washed-out blue of its sky, the breath one drew halfway up the hill that lounged against High Park, the sounds of voices echoing voices, the plain streets that led to avenues along which the houses were simple and true, and lanes that led past parks that flared as one passed them, leaving their impression of green and red and grey, the coloured metal of jungle gyms, swings and slides.)

He returned to his basement on Runnymede and, after eating a cheese sandwich, a handful of cherries, and a small container of vanilla-and-honey yoghurt, Baddeley went back to his novel, certain of the path he wanted to take, unconcerned as to whether it was the "right" path or not.

Days passed and he wrote in peace, unafraid of losing his way.

It was on his next visit to the Toronto Western that things grew more complicated. He had no trouble finding the room, and no sooner did he enter than God entered his being. But whereas his previous communions had been a pure ecstasy, this one was disturbing. While under God's influence, Baddeley suddenly experienced – as precisely as if he were actually there – a child being eaten by an alligator. He saw, felt, and heard. He imagined himself splattered with the blood that erupted from the child's mouth, his own shirt wet. He experienced both the child's terror *and* the happy patience of the alligator. He heard the child's last words

– I'll tell mom! I'll tell!

and tasted, along with the alligator, the gaminess of the prey, the copper-salt taste of its blood. He shared the creature's satisfaction at biting down hard, and for what seemed hours, Baddeley felt in equal measure the rightness of terror and the justice of hunger. He enjoyed the sweetness of human flesh. He experienced unspeakable fear and a savage complacency. His soul was torn in two and, finally, he cried out for mercy.

As soon as he cried out, Baddeley was brought back to himself. He was not brought back to the "real" world, however. He was once again in the ward with the mannequins. The three he could look at with impunity were comfortingly familiar. They were all versions of Anna Akhmatova, young and beautiful, middle-aged and sensual, old and dignified. The mannequin he was not meant to look at spoke.

– You mustn't cry out, it said. You must learn to bear it as I do.

There was no malice or unkindness. The words were said and then, in an instant, Baddeley was in a service elevator going down to where the ambulances came in.

To Baddeley's surprise, the character of his communion did not seem to affect the inspiration that followed. If anything, this disturbing episode was more inspiring than the ones that had preceded it. Baddeley set about writing as soon as he entered his apartment. He spent weeks immersed in the world of *Parakeet*. He resented anything that took him away from the work: eating, sleeping, washing. And yet, he felt a curious distance from the novel. For all the passion and dedication and inspiration that went into it, *Home is the Parakeet* seemed not to belong to him. Yes, he recognized the various bits of his life and thinking distributed through the work, but they were not the novel's raison d'être. Insofar as the work had, for Baddeley, a raison d'être, it was in the images and feelings that flooded from his imagination, a glorious release he could share with no one. In the end, the work was nothing but a shrine to his solitude.

(Why was he writing a novel, anyway? It had never been his ambition to write fiction.)

Baddeley began to understand what it was that had driven Avery Andrews to live away from the world. How had Andrews managed to spend so many years — so many decades — with the astounding visions *and* the inescapable solitude?

In fact, he came to appreciate Andrews' plight even more deeply in the year that followed. *Home is the Parakeet* was published, an event that should have brought him joy. In his previous life — that is, in his life before Avery Andrews — he'd imagined the moments of publication (the launch, the pleasure of meeting other writers, the admiration of strangers) as pure joy. But the launch of *Parakeet* was nothing like pleasure. It was dull and insignificant. It took place in a room filled with people he did not know, who did not know him. The food on offer was tasteless; his own nerves dulled the acuity of his senses. And beyond all that there was a feeling of fraudulence. *He* had not written the novel. *He* did not like novels. The thing had been given to him by a being whose only interest was in the supposed peace the invasion of Baddeley's psyche brought to it. A more hollow event than a book launch Baddeley could not imagine.

That is, he could not imagine anything more hollow until reviewers — and, to an extent, the public — decided they liked his book very much. *Home is the Parakeet* was, for the most part, warmly received. Baddeley had not been known as a novelist, so there were envious critics who would have preferred to knock him down a notch. But none could do so without ignoring the flagrant fact that something interesting was up with the novel. Yes, of course, a handful of reviewers stared down their own doubts, in order to deliver to the public a disdain they assumed, as Baddeley had once assumed, was what the public needed most. But few listened to them, save for readers who did not like novels in any case. Outdoing its publisher's expectations, *Parakeet* was what is called a bestseller. It was bought in great numbers and read by almost half of those who bought it.

This success, which meant nothing to Baddeley, was followed by a handful of surreal events that meant even less. He spoke to a thin, freckle-faced man on *Radio One*. On *Radio Two* he spoke to a stocky man with a Vandyke. And then he was invited to read at the "Festival of Authors," the invitation extended by the festival's artistic director who also invited Baddeley to a reception for a handful of writers who were at the festival that year.

The reception took place at a Korean restaurant on Bloor called *Fennel and Rue*. Its second floor is where food was served, but its first floor – a few steps down from street-level – was a tea house. To one side of the entrance was a barrel filled with rotting cabbage for kimchee. The tea house itself was predominantly wood – exposed beams, dark brown slats, knots and whorls like maddened veins. It was the kind of room that made you think of splinters until you actually touched the wood of the tables and benches and could feel them, smooth as polished stones. On offer in the tea house was tea: a varied and sometimes unexpected selection of flavours – grapefruit and cranberry; cranberry and walnut; orange and vanilla, etc. – served without any of the ritualistic fervour that sometimes poisoned tea houses.

Had he been alone, Baddeley would almost certainly have been comforted by the elegance of the room. But he was not alone. Little by little, the room filled with those for whom the reception was meant: writers, publishers, editors, and their various consorts. All were polite and all of them seemed kind. He should not have felt the least anxiety, but Baddeley was anxious from the beginning. He simply could not understand the connection between what he had gone through to write *Parakeet* and this bustle. He was conscious of how little he deserved to be in this place with these people. It seemed to him that everyone else — from the waitresses to the well-known — had better cause than he did to drink tea and eat the anise-flavoured biscuits that were passed around on silver platters.

Baddeley spoke briefly with a writer from the UK. And insulted him (or seemed to, though he hadn't meant any offense). He spoke even more briefly with an American writer, and seemed to insult him too. In any case, neither of his contemporaries had anything much to say and abandoned him, after politely smiling and turning away. So it was with almost everyone at the reception, even those who approached him first. The only exception was the slightly unwashed André Alexis, a writer whose work Baddeley despised. Alexis would not stop talking until Baddeley himself nodded politely and turned away, waving a hand in the air as if to signal to someone he'd seen on the other side of the room, though there was of course no one.

It occurred to Baddeley, as he turned away from Alexis, that it was possible — that it was perhaps true — that *all* the writers in the room felt as awkward and fraudulent as he did, that all of them were as unfit for society as he was. He dismissed this thought almost immediately, however. On the evidence, it could not be true that they *all* felt as he did, because the one thing his contemporaries did most consistently was to congregate at these dinners and launches, celebrations and memorials. Some of them, somewhere, had to be having something like fun. It was perverse to think otherwise.

The reception was, in a word, a damp squib. But the dinner upstairs was worse. The restaurant was not unappealing. It was high ceilinged, the walls above the white wainscoting a light blue. Framed and hanging on the walls were variously patterned, full-sized kimonos; perhaps a dozen of them in all. Tables of all sizes were distributed about the room. Half of the restaurant was reserved for the literary gathering. There were cards at the tables (white cards on which, in silvery, cursive script, names were printed) to indicate where one was supposed to sit. Someone had made a mistake, however, because when he found the card with his name, Baddeley saw that Gil Davidoff's card was at the place beside his. He was about to discreetly exchange his own card with that at another table when Gil himself appeared.

– Hey! said Davidoff. Where you been, Badds?

Davidoff was in his *tenue de chasse*: black jeans, a green, crewnecked sweater, a loose-fitting jacket with tweed patches at its elbows. He had new glasses: thick tortoise shelled rims, rectangular frames. His brown hair was boyishly dishevelled, as if he'd just stepped from bed, thrown a few things on and come to the reception at the pleading behest of the reception's organizers. Perhaps instinctively, Davidoff turned to look about the room thus affording Baddeley a view of what had been, at some point, a vaguely Keatsian profile but which was now a ruined, patrician vista: broken nose, protruding chin, gapped front teeth, greying hair, the face of a blowsy concierge.

– I didn't know you had a novel in you, Davidoff continued. I even heard it was okay. But you should be writing non-fiction. That's the thing these days. I'm writing about all the great television I'm making my son watch.

– That sounds interesting, said Baddeley.

– Plus chicks love it when you're an authority on something, said Davidoff.

Then, pausing for effect and turning to allow Baddeley a view of his hazel eyes, Davidoff said

– I don't know what I did to make you go all silent, Alexander, but I bet you miss me even more than I miss you, eh?

To Baddeley's knowledge, this was as close to an apology as Davidoff had ever come: a vague allusion to a vexing incident in which he may have played some part or other, though what that part was, exactly, Davidoff himself did not know.

– Yes, answered Baddeley.

– Well, I forgive you, said Davidoff. Let's not talk about this fit of yours again, okay buddy?

They sat down at their places. At the table with them were other literary lights. To Baddeley's left, there was the aging son of a late, great Canadian writer. The son, corpulent, his face as if carved from pink and grey butter, was himself a writer, but not a good one. To the son's left was his publicist, a woman who wore her hair severely pulled back. Her lipstick was of such a bright red and her face so heavily made up that she looked, to Baddeley, like a Raggedy Ann doll. To *her* left was a man with a hearing aid who smiled and said nothing. And to the left of the hearing aid was the hearing aid's wife.

In all the faces around all the tables there was not one that brought comfort to Baddeley. Davidoff's brought the opposite – a creeping despair at the thought that this man had once been his friend. And it was no doubt this incipient despair that further distorted the small world lodged in the throat of *Fennel and Rue*. Wherever Baddeley turned, things seemed slightly or even distinctly out of whack. At the table behind his, for instance, Margaret Atwood sat regally, her grey hair an afro of sorts, her cheekbones like half-buried golf balls. Nothing unusual there save that, after a moment, it seemed to Baddeley that there was something of the iguana to her, and no sooner did *that* thought occur to him than Atwood flicked out her pinkish tongue, the rest of her head as still as if it had not quite escaped from the wax in which it had been carved. Beside her, Graeme Gibson's neck grew so that he resembled a stork with thick glasses. In fact, all the necks in the room seemed to grow and sway vegetally, save, three tables away, Michael Ondaatje's. *His* neck shrank. His head bobbed up and down, looking like that of a strangely tufted raven.

Raggedy Ann's shrill voice interrupted Baddeley's reverie.

– There'd be no publishing in this country if it weren't for people like me, she said.

And it was then that the sounds of the menagerie assaulted him: implements on porcelain, women's laughter, the low laughter of their consorts and companions, the scraping of wood on wooden floors, and then coughing, shouting, and the clearing of throats. Here, faces came at him: Gowdy, Dewdney, Johnston, Lane. There, they settled back into the mire, anonymous again: Redhill, Crozier, Crosby, Toews. The lighting suddenly seemed sickly, the same colour as the excrescence from a garter snake. The hors d'oeuvres tasted of kerosene, and though the dinner was just starting, Baddeley had to leave.

– I'm going to be sick, he said.

– Well, don't do it on me, said Davidoff. I just washed this sweater.

Baddeley rose from the table and made as casual an exit as he could. He said nothing to anyone, leaving Davidoff to do any explaining that might be needed. He went down the stairs to the tea room, as if he were going out for a quick cigarette or something equally trivial. He imagined each and every patron in *Fennel and Rue* watching him as he retreated but, of course, not one of them noticed his departure.

Outside, the sun had not quite set. Somewhere in the west – beyond Parkdale, beyond Brown's Inlet – its reddish flash was almost gone. He was on Bloor Street near Christie. Looking east, the lights were bright and life seemed to quicken around Bathurst. Looking west, various shades of blue accumulated above the world, as if in a layered shot. To clear his mind, Baddeley decided to walk north to Dupont. He walked past Barton, Follis and Yarmouth. On one side of the street, Christie Pits, Fiesta Farms; on the other, Christie Station, and a mile's complement of modest houses.

It seemed to Baddeley that his soul caught up to him somewhere around Yarmouth. He looked over at the Spin Cycle Coin Laundry – above which, five irregularly spaced windows gave life to the red brick – and felt all of a sudden the solace that comes from being both somewhere and nowhere. He thought of Avery Andrews in the middle of Parkdale, – that is , in the middle of a neighbourhood to which he'd had no evident personal ties. "God," it seemed, was a drug that made company hard to bear.

The months that followed were a time of unshakable ambivalence. Baddeley did what his publisher expected of him: two readings and a brief interview in which he tried, unsuccessfully, to say what his novel "actually" meant. He tried to use his inspiration to write poetry. But poetry, even bad poetry, was beyond him. No words meant for poetry would come. What came, despite his resistance to it, was yet another novel. To make matters worse, the novel that came seemed little more than a variation on *Home is the Parakeet*. This one, *Over the Dark Hills*, was set in the heart of an African conflict, its protagonist called upon to lead a herd of elephants over mine-infested ground to freedom.

There was, of course, compensation. Writing while he was inspired was tonic. The hours would breeze by as he wrote about lands he'd never seen, animals he'd never touched, and people who brightly lived in the recesses of his psyche. *While* writing, he did not care *what* he was writing. Novel, fable, poem, recipe ... it was all the same. Disappointment came when he measured what he had written against his own ideals. First of all, there was, as far as Baddeley was concerned, the matter of fiction's inherent inferiority. When he compared his work to the genuinely sublime (Goethe's "Metamorphosis of Plants," say, or "Canto 3" of the *Inferno*), every word he'd written turned to ash.

Some time during the writing of *Over the Dark Hills*, at a moment when he was tempted to go back to the Toronto Western, Baddeley tried to reason himself away from his need for inspiration.

– I'm only writing fiction, he thought. I should be able to do this on my own.

It seemed to him that, having been a reviewer, he was familiar with "literature," familiar with its rules, variations, and tropes. He could push a character through memories and places as well as anyone else, surely. Davidoff had been doing it for years, and a less inspired writer there *could* not be. But five chapters into *Over the Dark Hills*, Baddeley no longer knew where to take the story. Should he kill off one of the elephants? Should his protagonist betray his fiancée? And to what terminal was *this* novel heading? He tried to think his way through his questions, but he simply did not trust his own instincts and reasons. So, he was left with a choice: he could go on writing and re-writing scenes until one of them felt right or he could return to the Toronto Western.

He returned to the hospital and, for the last time in his life, Baddeley found the room he was looking for at once. Anxious that "God" would overtake him before he could speak, Baddeley cried out as he entered the ward.

– Please, he asked, what are you?

– I am, said God, what you cannot imagine that imagines you.

– But are you God?

– That word has a trillion meanings, Alexander. I am and I am not what *you* mean by it.

– But why use *me*? asked Baddeley. What am I?

– You're the peace I seek endlessly, said God.

– But I don't think I'm as strong as Avery. I don't think I can … The Lord interrupted him.

– You're not Avery Andrews, Alexander. Your voyage is different.

– Do all writers go through this?

– Almost none of them do. Priests are much better at it.

– Did Avery see the kind of things I saw last time?

– Much worse, said God.

And took him to a terrifying place where he witnessed or, more exactly, participated in the murder of a family. Here, he was each of the three men who entered the family's home just before dawn. He could smell the last of the previous evening's supper. He experienced the killers' sense of righteousness, their exhilaration, their fear, their contempt for the ones they slaughtered. But he was also the three members of the family: father, mother, and twelve-year-old boy. His mind was as if partitioned in six and every moment experienced by each of his six selves was inescapable. He could not cry out, neither in righteousness nor fear. He experienced death three times and then found himself in an empty room in Radiography.

For a very long time after this, it did not matter to Alexander Baddeley what or who was at the heart of his ritual at Toronto Western: God, his own imagination, the devil, or the errant fumes of anaesthetic and soap. It did not matter whether the places he went were inside of him or not, whether the things he experienced were taking place, had taken place, or would take place. It did not seem to him that the words he dispersed over the pages of his Hilroy notebooks were any sort of compensation for this traumatic empathy.

Although his inspiration waned again towards the end of *Over the Dark Hills*, Baddeley chose one of the many endings that suggested itself, wrote it as plainly as he could and sent it off to his publisher, more or less unconcerned about the work's fate. Moreover, his lack of concern went unpunished. It seemed he alone noticed the flaws in the novel's ending. Those reviewers who actually finished the book assumed that the shift in tone towards the end was part of the novel's point. And the novel did well, allowing Baddeley to buy a house on Augusta, a house that was a short walk from the Toronto Western, though he hadn't been mindful of the hospital when he bought the place.

With the success of his novels, Baddeley had the life he wanted, a life of reading and reviewing, a life of seclusion and quiet in the heart of a city he had come to love.

More: it was a life that brought him closer to the work of the poet he still admired. Having been through some of what Avery Andrews had been through, it was now possible for Baddeley to rightly value Andrews' stamina, his persistence in the service of a "God" who was unstable and wayward. Knowing what Andrews had been through, Baddeley could now accept Andrews' poetry for what it was: the narrative of a man's withering in the presence of the sacred. Far from tarnishing Andrews' work, Baddeley's knowledge made the poems more precious to him. It also made him, he thought, the only man who knew (who would ever know) the true weight of Andrews' books.

And yet, this is not how the story of Baddeley's time with Avery Andrews ends.

Some eight years after the publication of *Over the Dark Hills*,

Alexander Baddeley should have been at peace with himself and the world. He was frugal. The money he made from his books was more than enough to keep him in Brussels sprouts and vanilla yoghurt. A movie was made of *Home is the Parakeet* – a good one, though it was unhappily named *Parakeets are Free!* – and there was talk of filming *Over the Dark Hills* as well. So, as far as anyone (himself included) could tell, Baddeley's future was not precarious. It was this very fact that began to weigh on him. He was not, he felt, *doing* enough with himself. Reviewing had become a habit, a reflex almost. It was no longer a proving ground or a necessary marketplace. He had grown comfortable, almost bourgeois and that thought troubled him.

Then, too, the pain he had experienced during the creation of his second novel had dissipated into the kind of memory of which one says, "Actually, it wasn't that bad, now that I think of it." He remembered, above all, the ecstasy of divine presence, the joy of exploring places in himself to which he did not otherwise have access. And then again, he was still young. Forty. Why should he not again experience the heights of inspiration?

So, one day, he went to the Toronto Western, warily but also hopefully, entering on Bathurst. The hospital was just that – a hospital. Spiritually speaking, there was nothing special about the place. At the entrance, it smelled of antiseptic and coffee and a host of evanescent things: perfume, leather, sweat, bread, urine, nail polish, rubbing alcohol ...

The sheer banality of the place was the most distressing thing about Baddeley's return. Whereas, in the past, he had gone *towards* something, towards a feeling, now it was as if he were in a place he'd never been before. The faces around him were, naturally, unfamiliar, but so was the way the light fell on the walls and the sound of shoes on the polished floors. Even the music playing – insistent and soft from somewhere above – was in a language he did not understand

– ... *e l'uomo sai chi e? Un certo Alexander che Manzoni fu* ...

Nowhere in this building of brick, concrete and glass did he feel anything like inspiration or the presence of "God". The building was not godless, exactly, but it was no more God-compassing than the Kensington market or the *Nova Era* bakery.

When a nurse stopped him to ask if she could help, he answered

– No, I was looking for a ward.

– Which one? she asked.

– 88A?

– I don't think there is an 88A, she said kindly. What seems to be the problem? Are you lost?

– No, no. Thank you very much, he answered.

But, of course, he *was* lost and, after a while, walking around the hospital was like walking in a forest when evening comes and one begins to suspect one has been going in circles.

Over the years that followed, Alexander Baddeley returned to the Toronto Western from time to time. He did not find "God" or inspiration or any such thing. However, the place saturated his consciousness and penetrated his dreams. And one night, while he was dreaming of an intersection in a city he did not recognize, a passerby of whom he asked directions smiled, pointed "west" and showed him what he held in his other hand: a stainless steel, kidney-shaped dish, four inches wide at it widest, eight inches long, and three inches deep. In the dish there were two white cotton squares of the kind used to swab skin before a needle is given. The swabs were side by side. One of them had a speck of blood on it.

– Oh, said Baddeley. I must be home.

And looking up he suddenly recognized the corner of Bathurst and Dundas, and saw that the passerby was not a stranger but, in fact, Avery Andrews, looking much as he'd looked when Baddeley saw him for the first time.

– I know, said Andrews.

Meaning that they were *both* home, a thought that filled Alexander Bertrand Baddeley with such relief he let himself sink deeper into the place from which all worlds come. And he woke the next morning feeling that he'd been — even if only briefly — as lucid as a human can be.

Toronto, 2011 – Ocala, 2012

Home is the Parakeet

&

AVERY ANDREWS' POETRY

WRITTEN BY HARRY MATHEWS

Colophon

Manufactured as the First Edition of *A*
in the fall of 2013 by BookThug.

Distributed in Canada
by the Literary Press Group
www.lpg.ca

Distributed in the United States
by Small Press Distribution
www.spdbooks.org

Shop online at
www.bookthug.ca

BOOK
PRODUCTION
WAR ECONOMY
STANDARD

Type + design by Jay MillAr
Copy edited by Ruth Zuchter